ONE GOOD DEED

DESERVES ANOTHER

This book is for Helen Evans . . .

Other fables retold by
Katherine Evans

The Mice That Ate Iron
A Bundle of Sticks
A Camel in the Tent
The Boy Who Cried Wolf
The Man, the Boy, and the Donkey
The Maid and Her Pail of Milk

ONE GOOD DEED DESERVES ANOTHER

retold and
illustrated by

Katherine Evans

Albert Whitman & Co. - Chicago

Early in the morning the sun came up
over the mountains at the edge of the world.
The blue mist faded away.

Juan, Carmelita, and little Pepe started
to market.
The trail to the village was long and steep.
Juan walked beside the burro.
Its back was loaded with serapes.
Behind walked Carmelita—on her head
she carried a basket of chickens.
Behind Carmelita walked Pepe.
Around his neck hung ropes of braided garlic.

The market was a busy place.
Juan sold his serapes, and Carmelita had
no trouble selling her chickens.
Even little Pepe sold his garlic buds
one by one until they were all gone.

Large pots of tamales and frijoles bubbled,
smelling of spices.
The family ate a fine dinner.
Then they started up the trail to their casa
in the mountains.

In the mountains Ruffo the Bandit
was hiding.
He had been hiding there all day.

On the other side of the mountain,
in the town, were signs that said,
Wanted: Ruffo the Bandit
1,000 Pesos for His Capture

Ruffo saw the little family coming up
the steep trail, tired after their day
at the market.
"Ha!" the bandit said to himself.
"They come from the market with pockets
full of pesos and a fine strong burro
on whose back I can ride away."

As the family came nearer, Ruffo backed
behind a tree.
He planned to jump out and take them
by surprise.
But—he tripped and his foot slipped
over the edge of the cliff.

As he fell, Ruffo was caught by a tree.
There he hung.
He looked far below and was frightened.
"Help, help!" he called.

Hearing the calls, Juan looked over
the side of the cliff.
"Only have courage, amigo," he shouted.
"We will help you."

Carmelita took off her long rebozo,
and Juan let it down to the bandit.
Ruffo held one end and Juan, Carmelita,
and little Pepe pulled and pulled.
At last they pulled Ruffo safely up
over the cliff.

"Hand over your money and the burro," growled Ruffo when he was back on the road.

"This is not right!" cried poor Juan. "It is wrong to repay us this way."

"That may be so," said Ruffo, "but I am hungry and I must get away."

"Before you rob us, let us ask someone else for his opinion," begged Juan.

"It will be of little help, but I will give you one chance," said the bandit. "If we find anyone, we will ask."

With the bandit at their backs,
Juan, Carmelita, and little Pepe
had only gone a short way along the trail
when they saw a boy resting by the road.

"Come here, amigo," called Juan.
"We want your opinion to settle a dispute."

"What is the trouble?" asked the boy.
"I am only a boy and whatever I say
can be of little use."

Juan told how they had pulled Ruffo up
over the cliff and saved his life.
In return, Ruffo wanted to rob them.

"But I say it is not right to return
good with evil," said Juan.

The bandit, speaking in turn, explained
that he had hurt his leg and had no money.
Now Juan wanted to leave him by the road
with no way to get over the mountains.

"What you tell is not enough," said the boy.
"I must study the case before I can answer.
Now just where did you find this man when
he called for help?
Show me how he was caught in a tree.
It may be that he was not really in danger.
It may be it was only a trap to rob you."

"Not really in danger?" yelled the bandit.
"I'll show you what danger is!"
He was so angry that he jumped over the cliff
into the branches of the tree below.

The boy looked down where Ruffo hung.
"Is that really the way that you were caught?"
he asked.
"You called for help because you could not
climb up over the edge of the cliff?"

"Yes!" said the bandit.
"As you can see, it is impossible."

"Is that really the way you found him?"
the boy asked Juan, Carmelita, and Pepe.

"It is," they answered.

"Then," said the boy, "the situation is now better than when I found it. That is my opinion."

"It is not right to leave me here,"
yelled Ruffo.

"If good is repaid with evil, then
this time evil brings good,"
said the boy.

"You have saved us from being
robbed," said Juan gratefully.

"May God reward you for your
good deed," said Carmelita.

On the trail, clatter of hoofs was heard.
A caballero on a black horse galloped up.
"Have you seen the bandit?" he asked.
"He is loose in the hills.
A thousand pesos is offered for his capture."

They all looked at each other.

Juan said, "Senor, I can lead you to him.
Due to this young man, he hangs in a tree
over the edge of a cliff."

And so Ruffo was pulled up on the road.
He knew that he could not escape.
Down the mountain to the village he went,
tied to the end of a rope.

In the village everyone gathered to see
the wicked bandit.
In the Plaza the boy was given his reward,
one thousand pesos.
He bought tamales for all his friends.

Pedro and Carlos in their big sombreros
brought out their guitars.
They played and sang such gay songs
that everyone sang.

All but Ruffo.

Looking through the bars of his jail,
he growled, "Caramba!"

Repaying good with evil is the theme of a number of animal tales told by Indians of the Southwest and Mexico.

Katherine Evans in retelling such a story in *One Good Deed Deserves Another* leaves her villain behind bars. But once, the story ran, Snake was caught beneath a stone. When Rabbit rescued him, Snake threatened to eat Rabbit. A poor reward indeed! Fortunately Coyote, trickster in so many tales, happened along. He suggested that Rabbit and Snake assume the positions they had had at first meeting. This meant that Snake was again pinned beneath the stone—an appropriate reward for his own treatment of Rabbit, said Coyote.